CAPTAIN RAPTOR and the SPACE PIRATES

KEVIN O'MALLEY and PATRICK O'BRIEN
Illustrations by PATRICK O'BRIEN

Walker & Company  New York

IN THE MISTY SKIES ABOVE THE PLANET JURASSICA, A *DARK AND SINISTER SHAPE* IS SEEN MOVING AMONG THE CLOUDS.

SUDDENLY . . .
BOOM!
A CANNON ROARS OVERHEAD.

AMID THE FIRE AND SMOKE, THE PIRATE SHIP *BLACKROT* DESCENDS TO THE GROUND.

SMASHING THROUGH A HEAVY DOOR, THE RAMPAGING ROGUES FIND THE FAMOUS ***JEWELS OF JURASSICA.***

WEIGHED DOWN WITH TREASURE, THE PIRATES DASH BACK INTO THEIR SHIP AND BLAST OFF, LEAVING THE PALACE IN RUINS.

"THOSE PIRATES MUST BE STOPPED!" ROARS THE PRESIDENT.
"BUT SIR, WHAT CAN WE DO?"
"I'LL TELL YOU WHAT WE DO. WE CALL . . ."

"...CAPTAIN RAPTOR!"

CAPTAIN RAPTOR ASSEMBLES HIS FEARLESS CREW:

BLASTOFF!

CAPTAIN RAPTOR'S TRUSTY PILOT, LIEUTENANT THREETOE, IS AT THE CONTROLS AS THE *MEGATOOTH* **RACES THROUGH SPACE**, FOLLOWING THE *BLACKROT*'S ION TRAIL.

THROUGH THE STAR CLUSTER OF REPTILIUS 4, FAR AROUND THE PERILUS NEBULA, THE *MEGATOOTH* CHASES THE FLEEING PIRATES.

AT LAST, CAPTAIN RAPTOR SPOTS THE *BLACKROT*, DRIFTING WITHOUT POWER NEAR A SMALL, UNKNOWN MOON.

"CAPTAIN," SAYS THREETOE, "SEE THAT SMOKE? THEIR SHIP IS DAMAGED. ***NOW'S OUR CHANCE! I'M GOING IN!***"
"NO, ***PULL BACK,*** THREETOE. ***I SMELL A TRAP!***"

TOO LATE! BLAM! BLAM! BOOM! THE MEGATOOTH IS BLASTED WITH TONS OF MOLTEN LEAD.

CAPTAIN RAPTOR AND HIS CREW GO *SPINNING UNCONTROLLABLY* TOWARD THE ROCKY MOON.
COULD THIS BE *THE END* OF CAPTAIN RAPTOR?

"I CAN'T CONTROL HER, CAPTAIN! *WE'RE GOING TO CRASH!*"
"NOT ON MY WATCH, THREETOE!"

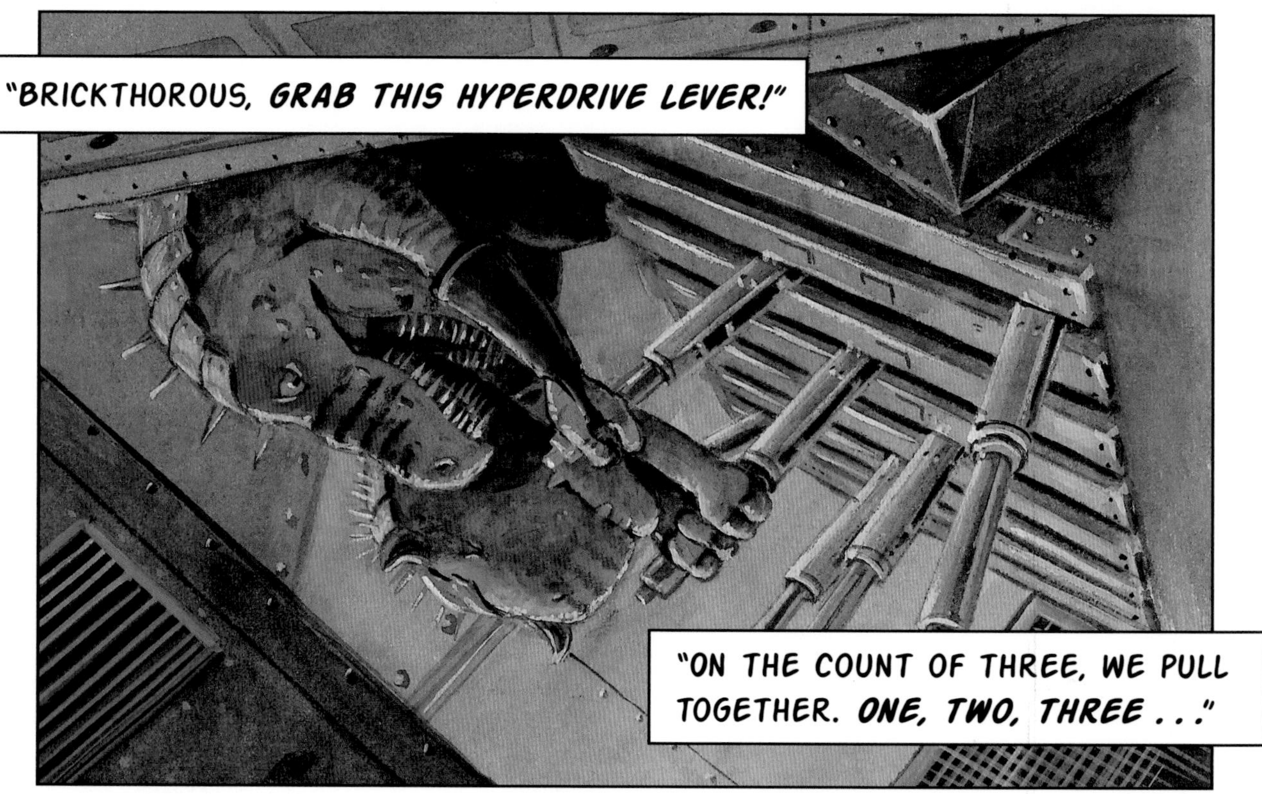
"BRICKTHOROUS, *GRAB THIS HYPERDRIVE LEVER!*"
"ON THE COUNT OF THREE, WE PULL TOGETHER. *ONE, TWO, THREE . . .*"

AT THE LAST MOMENT, CAPTAIN RAPTOR AND BRICKTHOROUS MANAGE TO CONTROL THE SPIN AND GET HER NOSE UP. THE *MEGATOOTH* HITS ***HARD***, THEN SCRAPES AND SLIDES TO A STOP.

THE CAPTAIN AND CREW STAGGER OUT ONTO A BARREN LANDSCAPE.
"STRANGE, THIS MOON DOESN'T SHOW UP ON ANY OF MY SPACE MAPS. AND IT SEEMS TO BE COMPLETELY DESERTED."

ANGLEOPTEROUS EXAMINES THE SHIP'S ENGINES. "CAPTAIN, OUR PLUTONIC SERVOSCOPE IS SHATTERED. THERE'S NO WAY TO FIX IT—WE DON'T HAVE THE PARTS. I'M AFRAID WE'RE STUCK HERE."

"WE'LL GET OFF THIS ROCK, OR MY NAME ISN'T CAPTAIN RAP—" SUDDENLY, CAPTAIN RAPTOR *SPRINGS UP* AND RUSHES OFF INTO THE BUSHES.

HE RETURNS, DRAGGING A WRETCHED CREATURE IN RAGGED CLOTHES.
"I CAUGHT THIS SCOUNDREL SPYING ON US!"

"*I* AM CAPTAIN RAPTOR OF THE PLANET JURASSICA. NOW, WHO ARE YOU?"

"WHY, I CAN RIG UP THAT OLD BARGE OF YERS AND HAVE HER ALL SHIPSHAPE IN NO TIME, CAP'N. BUT YOU'LL HAVE TO BE TAKIN' ME WITH YA WHEN YA BLAST OUT OF HERE."

CAPTAIN RAPTOR STARES INTO SCALAWAG'S BEADY EYES, THEN SAYS, "VERY WELL."

TRUE TO HIS WORD, SCALAWAG REPAIRS THE BROKEN SHIP.

THE *MEGATOOTH* ENTERS THE NEBULA, A MYSTERIOUS CLOUD OF GAS AND COSMIC DUST.

ROBOKRON!
THE *GIANT ROBOTIC SPACE BEAST* CIRCLES THE *MEGATOOTH*, ITS ***SPIKY JAWS*** OPEN WIDE!
"***TAKE THAT!***" SHOUTS BRICKTHOROUS, FIRING A BLASTOCANNON. BUT THE BURST JUST ***BOUNCES OFF*** THE MONSTER'S METAL SKIN.

COULD *THIS* BE THE END OF CAPTAIN RAPTOR?

"CAP'N!" SHOUTS SCALAWAG. "I'VE TANGLED WITH THIS MONSTER BEFORE. IF YOU CAN GET TO THE ELECTRIC PANEL ON ITS NECK, YOU CAN CUT ITS POWER LINE. THAT'S THE ONLY WAY TO DEFEAT IT!"
CAPTAIN RAPTOR CLIMBS OUT THE HATCH, LEAPS ONTO THE ROBOKRON'S BACK, AND CLAMBERS UP TO ITS NECK. OPENING THE ELECTRIC PANEL, HE SEES DOZENS OF WIRES. WHICH ONE TO CUT?

WITH THE ROBOKRON'S TEETH SLOWLY CRUSHING THE MEGATOOTH, CAPTAIN RAPTOR REACHES IN AND YANKS OUT EVERYTHING HE SEES.

THERE'S A SHOWER OF SPARKS, AND THEN A HUGE ELECTRIC JOLT HURTLES HIM BACK ONTO THE MEGATOOTH.

THE ROBOKRON GOES LIMP AND BEGINS TO FALL JUST AS CAPTAIN RAPTOR ***DIVES*** INTO THE *MEGATOOTH*'S HATCH.
"***STEP ON IT, THREETOE!*** LET'S SEE WHAT THIS SHIP CAN DO!"

THE *MEGATOOTH* ***ZOOMS*** OUT FROM BELOW THE FALLING MONSTER, THEN ***SPEEDS*** BACK THROUGH SPACE TO JURASSICA.

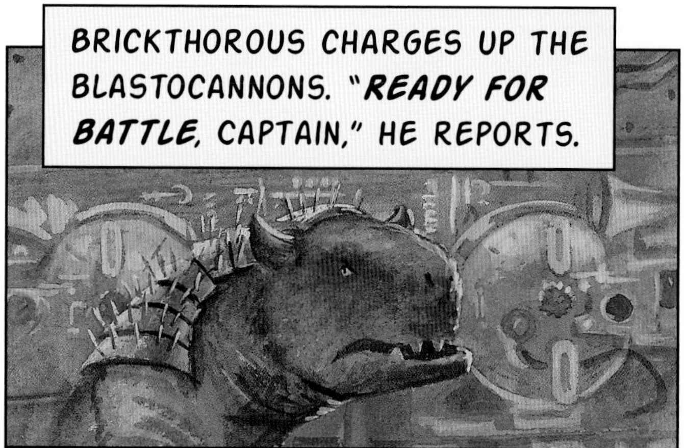

SOON, THE PIRATE SHIP EMERGES FROM THE MISTS.

SCALAWAG TURNS ON THE RADIO COMMUNICATOR AND SHOUTS AT THE PIRATES, "***LET ME THROUGH, YA SCURVY DOGS!*** BLOODY BART SCALAWAG HAS RETURNED! AND YOU'LL NOT GET RID O' ME THIS TIME!"

"***WE CAN'T TAKE MUCH MORE OF THIS,***" SHOUTS THREETOE. "THE *BLACKROT'S* TOO BIG FOR US. ***WE'RE SHOT FULL OF HOLES!***"

IS ***THIS*** THE END OF CAPTAIN RAPTOR?

"CAPTAIN, WE'RE DONE FOR!"
"RELAX, THREETOE. I NEVER REALLY TRUSTED SCALAWAG. SO BEFORE THE BATTLE I PACKED A SMALL GOING-AWAY PRESENT INTO OUR SHUTTLE CRAFT. I THINK THAT SCALAWAG WILL FIND IT QUITE . . . EXPLOSIVE."

"IF YOU WOULD KINDLY PUSH THIS RED BUTTON . . ."
"IT WOULD BE MY PLEASURE, CAPTAIN."

THE BACK OF THE *BLACKROT* IS TAKEN OFF BY THE EXPLOSION. THE SHIP *SPIRALS* DOWN TO THE PLANET BELOW.

THE PIRATES TUMBLE OUT, DAZED AND DEFEATED. TONS OF TREASURE SPILL ONTO THE GROUND.
THE DINOSAURS OF JURASSICA CAN REST EASY NOW. CAPTAIN RAPTOR AND HIS FEARLESS CREW HAVE *SAVED THE DAY* AGAIN.
"SCALAWAG, YOU'VE LOST YOUR SHIP AGAIN. BUT THIS TIME YOU WON'T BE LEFT ALL ALONE ON A DESERT PLANET. YOU'LL BE SPENDING PLENTY OF TIME WITH YOUR CREW—*IN PRISON*."

"THREETOE, LET'S FIND A CORNER OF SPACE THAT'S *OFF THE MAPS*. WE'RE IN FOR MORE ADVENTURES!"
"ONWARD TO THE STARS!"

FIRST PUBLISHED IN THE UNITED STATES OF AMERICA IN 2007 BY WALKER PUBLISHING COMPANY, INC.
DISTRIBUTED TO THE TRADE BY HOLTZBRINCK PUBLISHERS

FOR INFORMATION ABOUT PERMISSION TO REPRODUCE SELECTIONS FROM THIS BOOK,
WRITE TO PERMISSIONS, WALKER & COMPANY, 175 FIFTH AVENUE, NEW YORK, NEW YORK 10010

LIBRARY OF CONGRESS CATALOGING-IN-PUBLICATION DATA
O'MALLEY, KEVIN.
CAPTAIN RAPTOR AND THE SPACE PIRATES / KEVIN O'MALLEY AND PATRICK O'BRIEN ;
ILLUSTRATIONS BY PATRICK O'BRIEN.
P. CM.
SUMMARY: CAPTAIN RAPTOR AND THE CREW OF THE *MEGATOOTH* ARE CALLED BACK INTO ACTION TO SAVE THE PLANET JURASSICA FROM ROGUE SPACE PIRATES.
ISBN-13: 978-0-8027-9571-7 • ISBN-10: 0-8027-9571-4 (HARDCOVER)
ISBN-13: 978-0-8027-9572-4 • ISBN-10: 0-8027-9572-2 (REINFORCED)
[1. DINOSAURS—FICTION. 2. PIRATES—FICTION. 3. SCIENCE FICTION.] I. O'BRIEN, PATRICK, ILL. II. TITLE.
PZ7.O526CSP 2007 [E]—DC22 2006101182

BOOK DESIGN BY PATRICK O'BRIEN
ART CREATED WITH WATERCOLOR AND GOUACHE
TYPESET IN ACTION MAN

VISIT WALKER & COMPANY'S WEB SITE AT WWW.WALKERYOUNGREADERS.COM

PRINTED IN CHINA
4 6 8 10 9 7 5 3 (HARDCOVER)
2 4 6 8 10 9 7 5 3 (REINFORCED)

ALL PAPERS USED BY WALKER & COMPANY ARE NATURAL, RECYCLABLE PRODUCTS MADE FROM WOOD GROWN IN WELL-MANAGED FORESTS. THE MANUFACTURING PROCESSES CONFORM TO THE ENVIRONMENTAL REGULATIONS OF THE COUNTRY OF ORIGIN.